Fearless Fiona

The Mystery of the Great Stone Haggis
and The Rolls-Royce Racket Mystery

Karen Wallace

Illustrated by Judy Brown

To another Fearless Fiona, with thanks

Published by
Happy Cat Books
An imprint of Catnip Publishing Ltd
Islington Business Centre
3-5 Islington High Street
London N1 9LQ

This edition first published 2007
1 3 5 7 9 10 8 6 4 2

Text copyright © Karen Wallace, 2007
Illustrations copyright © Judy Brown, 2007

The moral right of the author/ illustrator has been asserted

A CIP catalogue record for this book is available from
the British Library

ISBN 978-1-905117-44-4

Printed in Poland

www.catnippublishing.co.uk

Contents

Also by Karen Wallace in Happy Cat Books

The Mothproof Hall Mystery
Spooky Beasts

The Mystery of the Great Stone Haggis

Chapter One

"Whaddyamean your hotel's full of people pretending to be haggises?" Deadline Metalpress, editor of the *Daily Screamer*, yelled to Crystal Rainbird, manageress of the Tartan Traveller Hotel.

"Whaddyamean, you don't know?"

he screamed. He banged down the
telephone. Then he banged his head on
his desk.

His secretary opened the door.

"Did you bang, sir?" she asked
sweetly.

"I certainly did," said Deadline
Metalpress. "Get me Fearless Fiona,
fast!"

Fearless Fiona Metalpress was
a part-time reporter on the *Daily
Screamer*. She had a nose for a story
that would leave a bloodhound
howling. Deadline Metalpress used to
say she was born with a notebook in
her hand.

When she was older, he gave her a portable telephone. "I might need you in a hurry," he had said.

Now that phone was ringing.

"Fearless," yelled Deadline Metalpress. He had a voice like a rock rattling in an oil drum.

"There's something funny going on at the Tartan Traveller Hotel."

Fearless's heart missed a beat.

"That's where we're staying," she said. "What's happening?"

"It's full of people wearing deep-sea diving suits, calling themselves haggises," shouted her father. "Find out what's going on. I need a good story for the *Scottish Screamer*."

"You can count on me, Chief, er, Dad," said Fearless Fiona.

And she never let him down. Even when it wasn't easy. Like now, when she was in Scotland on holiday with her mother who only liked newspapers when they were wrapped around fish and chips . . .

Three hours later, Mrs Metalpress thought about the cup of tea she had been offered at the Tartan Traveller Hotel. How it had been snatched from her hand.

How she had been rushed down to the quay and loaded into an old wooden boat.

Something about a story. She
didn't know and she didn't care.
Now she sat, huddled like a wet
hen, watching the cold waters of
Loch Haggis slop over the side.
"Fiona Jane!" she shrieked.
"Your skirt will be ruined!"
Fearless Fiona looked at the

slimy pink cloth that covered her
knees. It was not the sort of thing a
part-time reporter would normally
be seen dead in. She thought of the
cut-off shorts she just happened to be
wearing underneath.

Splot! A bucket of salt water landed
in her lap.

Mightie McDougie, boatman and guide, winked under his curly grey eyebrows. "Would ye mind if I used the skirt as a wee sail?" he asked.

"Help yourself," said Fearless.

Mrs Metalpress groaned and took out her knitting. A minute later, the little boat picked up speed and they shot around a headland into a bay.

On the shore, halfway up the mountain, was a grey house with turrets that looked like pepper grinders. In front of the house stood an enormous shiny boulder.

Fearless Fiona stared at it. "It looks just like a—"

"The Great Stone Haggis!" cried Mightie McDougie, waving his arms. "It guards the entrance to Haggis House." Then he pointed to the water. "And there lies the key."

Fearless snapped open her notebook. "OK, Mightie," she said. "What's the story?"

Mightie McDougie's eyes glittered. "One hundred years ago to this very day, the last Haggis locked the door and threw the key into the loch."

Fearless looked out across the water.
It was full of boats and people in
diving gear. "So why are all these
people here?" she asked.

"The saying goes that the rightful Haggis heir must find the key by midnight tonight," said Mightie McDougie. "Or else Haggis House, the loch and land will be sold."

"Does anyone want to buy it?" asked Fearless.

"A scoundrel called Nigel Pug," said Mightie McDougie. "He's staying at the Tartan Traveller – waiting like a vulture."

"Who is the rightful Haggis heir?" asked Fearless.

Mightie McDougie pointed to the people in the water.

"Who knows?" he said. "They all say they are called Haggis. But there is one thing for certain."

"What?" asked Fearless.

"The peacocks have returned

to Haggis House," said Mightie McDougie. "It is a sure sign. A rightful Haggis is amongst us. Only the key is still lost."

"I see," said Fearless, slowly.

"Sounds as clear as mud to me," grumbled Mrs Metalpress. Her feet were wet and the snatched cup of tea was preying on her mind.

"Plees," said a foreign-sounding voice.

A diver surfaced in the grey water beside the boat. He had an enormous moustache that hung like wet rope on either side of his mouth.

"My name is 'Aggis," he said. "Izz ziss where I find ze key to ze house?"

Mightie McDougie pointed to the bottom of the loch.

"Zank you," said the diver, and disappeared.

Fearless Fiona looked out beyond the strange shiny boulder to the turrets of Haggis House. Hundreds of peacocks were perched on the roof, their tail feathers spread in a shimmering fan of blue eyes. High up on the mountain behind them, a stag raised its head, its antlers sharp-edged against the sky.

She snapped her notebook shut. There was a determined set to her chin and a look in her eye that meant business. Haggis House would be saved. Fearless Fiona was on the case.

Chapter Two

Nigel Pug, chairman of Rodent-Resources Limited, smiled at himself in the mirror. Two greedy eyes in a greasy face smiled back. Nigel Pug was pleased with himself.

The key to Haggis House hadn't been found. Everything would be his at midnight. It was all going according to plan.

He unpacked his suitcase and pulled on a shiny jacket. He looked at his reflection again. "You look smug, Pug," he whispered. Then he walked downstairs to dinner.

Crystal Rainbird stood in the dining room of the Tartan Traveller and folded the last dark-brown napkin into the shape of a worm. The dining room was her pride and joy.

Deer heads sprouting dried flowers instead of antlers were dotted on the purple walls. Heart-shaped mirrors hung between pink satin curtains.

Crystal Rainbird liked to maintain high standards. In the

evenings she wore an orange silk pyjama suit and lots of green eye make-up. She patted her stiff yellow hair. Her eyelashes looked like two spiders crawling out of a swamp.

Crystal and her husband Clarence had put a lot of work into making the Tartan Traveller a nice place for nice people to stay. She pursed her scarlet lips. Now that horrible little man, Nigel Pug, was trying to ruin everything.

"Little beast," she said out loud.

"I beg your pardon, Mrs Rainbird," said Mrs Metalpress.

"Little beast," said Crystal again.

Fearless Fiona sat down on her chair.

"Who is?" she asked.

"Nigel Pug, that's who," said Crystal Rainbird, throttling one of her napkin worms.

"Isn't he the one who wants to buy Haggis House?" asked Fearless.

"That's him," snarled Crystal Rainbird. "He wants to bulldoze the house and build the world's biggest edible dormouse factory all along the loch and right up to our front terrace."

"Ugh!" said Fearless Fiona. "Do people really eat dormice?"

"They do," said Crystal Rainbird. "I read about it in the *Crunchy Lunches* cookbook."

Mrs Metalpress sniffed. She didn't approve of Nigel Pug – ever since she had caught him kissing his reflection in a hotel mirror. "Some people will do anything for attention," she said.

She shuddered delicately. "Let's

change the subject. What's for supper?"

"Salmon or spaghetti, seaweed or side salad," said Crystal Rainbird. "The salmon comes from Loch Haggis and the spaghetti comes in different colours, so you can weave your own tartan before you eat it."

Mrs Metalpress's eyes lit up.

"Ooo," she said. "I'll have the spag."

"Salmon for me, please," said Fearless Fiona.

A tall man wearing a false beard and a cowboy hat threw himself down on a spindly gold chair beside them. "Hi," he said. "I'm Slimeball Haggis, one of the Texas Haggises. Pleased to meetya."

He pointed to a blonde woman in a tight black skirt and glitter T-shirt. "This here is Cindy Haggis. She's my, um, grandmother."

"Sister, you idiot," hissed the blonde woman.

"Hey, waitress," said Slimeball Haggis. "Two Cokes and a hot dog for my, um, aunt."

The blonde woman rolled her eyes. Crystal Rainbird made a noise like a camel choking. Fearless Fiona looked up. She had seen these so-called Haggises in diving suits out on the loch.

"Are you on holiday?" she asked.

"Not exactly," said Slimeball. "We're looking for something my great-great-grandaddy dropped by mistake."

Cindy Haggis glared at him with eyes like toothpicks. Then she glared at Fearless.

"I saw you on the loch with a notebook in your hand," she said.

"What were you looking at?"

"Just the view," said Fearless in her sweetest voice. She turned away and pretended to read her menu. She didn't like Slimeball or Cindy one little bit.

She looked around the dining room. A man in a bowler hat was talking to a budgie in a cage on his table. Next to him a woman dressed in a leopard-skin was eating her supper with a dagger. Fearless had seen them both out on the loch and she had looked in the hotel's register book. Both of them were called Haggis.

Fearless Fiona sighed. If the key couldn't be found, how was she going to prove who was the rightful Haggis and stop Nigel Pug building

his disgusting dormouse factory? If only she knew what the peacocks knew as they waited for the rightful Haggis on the grey turrets of Haggis House.

A podgy little man stood a few feet away. Nigel Pug was purple in the face and was wearing a tie with a picture of himself in a chef's hat carrying a dormouse on a silver tray. "This is outrageous!" he squealed. "I want that table."

"That's my table," growled Mightie McDougie from behind him. "You oily vulture."

Slimball Haggis jumped to his feet. "Oil!" he yelped. "Who said anything about oil?"

"Shut up," hissed Cindy and kicked him in the shins.

Fearless saw them exchange a shifty look.

At that moment Crystal Rainbird arrived with their supper. There was a whole salmon on her plate.

"I can't eat all of that," she whispered to her mother.

"Eat half of it, then," said Mrs Metalpress, already putting what looked like a scarf into her mouth. "We'll send the rest home to your father."

Fearless Fiona pressed down the sharp knife.

It went clink!

"Don't play with your food, darling," said Mrs Metalpress, starting on a shawl.

"The knife won't go through," said Fearless.

"It's just a bone," said her mother.

Fearless opened up the salmon. There was no bone. Inside the salmon was a long rusty key with a strange haggis-shaped lump at one end! Fearless Fiona's heart thumped in her chest. She had found the missing key!

Now she was the only person who could save Haggis House.

She thought of all the people who were calling themselves Haggis. One of them must be the rightful heir. But who was it?

She shivered as she thought what could happen if she gave the key to the wrong one.

Around her, the dining room was

full of the sound of knives and forks scraping on china. She moved her napkin beside her plate and was just about to hide the key inside it when Mrs Metalpress stared across the table.

"An old key," she shrieked.

"Darling! It must be a Scottish custom. We put money in Christmas puddings. They put keys in fish!"

The scraping of knives and forks stopped.

Not a chair squeaked.

Fearless Fiona looked up. Everyone was looking at her.

Only Mightie McDougie
went on eating, but there was
no scraping sound, only a steady
slurping. (Because Mightie
McDougie ate spaghetti with his
fingers.)

CRASH!

A gold chair broke in half.

Nigel Pug leapt across the room
and grabbed at the key.

Quick as a flash, Mightie
McDougie threw a handful of
spaghetti at him. Pug opened his
mouth to yell but found himself
gargling instead. He banged into
Fearless Fiona's table. The key flew
into the air and fell in a long curve
towards the floor.

The entire dining room gasped as

Slimeball produced a magnet
out of his cowboy hat.
CLUNK!
The key whistled across the table
and stuck to the magnet!
"Oh no you don't," shouted Mrs

Metalpress. "That's my souvenir." And she grabbed his false beard – which turned out not to be false at all – and thwacked him on the head with her handbag.

Slimeball buckled over, clutching his chin and yowling horribly. The magnet hit the floor and the key bounced into the white hairy carpet.

Fearless Fiona saw her chance.

Cindy saw hers, too. But she was wearing a tight skirt and Fearless was in her cat suit. Fearless got there first. As she ran from the dining room she caught Mightie McDougie's eye.

"It's up to you, lassie!" he cried. "Only you can save Haggis House now!"

Chapter Three

Fearless Fiona raced across the lawn
to the bike shed. A bright moon
hung in the sky, making the pine
trees look huge and threatening.

The sound of shouting and
breaking china floated across the
lawn.

As fast as she could, she clipped

a mining light to her helmet and
switched it on. Immediately a pool
of yellow light spread across the
dark, wet grass.

She climbed on her mountain bike and pointed it into the trees. The light lit up a narrow stony path in front of her. She knew it led down the hill and all the way along the loch until it stopped beside the great stone haggis.

Fearless Fiona, star reporter of the *Daily Screamer*, patted the top pocket of her white leather cat suit. The ancient iron key was securely zipped in. She took a deep breath and set off down the path to Haggis House.

There must be a clue inside, she told herself. I have to give the key to somebody at midnight. This is my last chance to identify the rightful Haggis.

As she pedalled through the black night, Fearless thought of Nigel Pug and his disgusting plans. Of the shifty look between Slimeball and

Cindy. She just couldn't believe that he was the rightful Haggis or that Cindy was his sister. Maybe it was the man in the bowler hat. Or even Clarence Rainbird. She had overheard Mrs Rainbird saying that Clarence had changed his name years before because she had refused to be called Crystal Haggis.

Suddenly the night was full of squawking. Hundreds of peacocks flew down from the roof and spread

their tails in huge blue-eyed fans behind them. The ground was covered with feathers.

Fearless Fiona parked her bike against the Great Stone Haggis and walked up to the front door of the house. The key turned first time. She took a deep breath and went in.

A hundred years is a long time. Haggis House smelt like a cross between an old tennis shoe and a goat's breakfast. In the bright pool of the mining light, Fearless could see cobwebs as thick as shawls and hear the scurrying of tiny feet as the furry inhabitants of the house scattered to their holes. She walked along a short hall and down a flight of steps into a cellar. Might as well work from the bottom up, she told herself.

There was a strange smell in the cellar and the floor was sticky as if someone had dropped a tin of syrup. Fearless aimed the light at her feet. She was standing in some sort of black gooey stuff. She bent down and sniffed it.

It was what Texans like Slimeball called Black Gold or Texas Tea—it was oil!

There must be an oil well underneath the house, thought Fearless in amazement. That meant whoever inherited Haggis House would be a millionaire! She remembered how Slimeball had jumped when he heard the word oil. That's what the shifty look had been about. Slimeball and Cindy had known about the well and had been planning to keep the fortune for themselves.

Fearless felt for the key in her top pocket. Now there was even more at stake than the house and the land. The rightful Haggis must be found! And fast!

She raced up the stairs into what looked like a huge dining room. The table was still laid for a dinner one hundred years ago. At one end there was an enormous serving platter with a big crusty lump on it. It looked like a fossilized haggis.

Fearless Fiona bent over and gave

it a quick sniff. Ugh! It smelt like one, too!

Two candlesticks the size of small trees stood in the middle of the table. There were candles still in them. Fearless found a box of matches in one of her pockets. She climbed on to the table and lit them.

All around her the walls were hung with portraits of Haggises. There was a Haggis in a long curling wig, a Haggis on horseback and a Haggis holding a telescope to his eye. There was even a Haggis in a ballgown clutching a monkey in a jewelled collar.

Fearless Fiona stared at them all. There was something peculiar about the portraits. In every one the face was grinning. But more than that. In every grin there was a big gap between the front teeth.

It was the clue she had been looking for. Fearless Fiona thought quickly. What I have to do is make all the people calling themselves Haggis, laugh. The one with the gap between their teeth is the rightful heir.

It was a good plan. There was only one problem. Even though Fearless Fiona was a star reporter, that didn't mean she was any good at standing up in front of a whole lot of people and telling a funny joke.

A gust of wind wobbled the candle flame. Fearless Fiona began to feel nervous. She didn't even know any funny jokes!

"FEARLESS! FEARLESS!" boomed a voice in the empty house.

Fearless Fiona nearly jumped out of her skin. She turned and the bright light on her helmet caught Mightie McDougie, standing in the door waving a sword.

"Quick," he yelled. "They're coming. The vultures are coming. What are we going to do?"

"Light every candle we can find," said Fearless Fiona. "I'm ready for them." She paused. "There's just one thing . . ."

Mightie McDougie stared at her,

wild-eyed and shaking. "What is it?" he cried.

"Have you heard any good jokes recently?" asked Fearless Fiona, grimly.

There was a tremendous screeching and squawking. It sounded as if all the peacocks had stepped on each other's tails. The next minute, Nigel Pug and Slimeball stumbled into the room. Behind them came Crystal and Clarence Rainbird, Mrs Metalpress, Cindy Haggis and all the other Haggises.

Mightie McDougie turned to Fearless. He shouted, "Do you know the one about—"

"You can't stop me now," screamed Nigel Pug, pushing past him.

"Rodent–Resources—"

"Can run up a drainpipe," yelled Slimeball. "I've got plans for this here place and you're not in them."

"What are you talking about?" screamed Nigel Pug.

Fearless Fiona looked at her watch. It was ten seconds to midnight and she still couldn't think of a joke. Not even a bad joke.

Her mind was blank. The key felt heavy in her pocket. She had to give it to someone before midnight. But who? Who was the rightful Haggis?

With a huge leap, Mightie McDougie jumped on to the table. "Knock, knock," he yelled.

"Who's there?" cried Fearless.

"Sonya" yelled Mightie McDougie.

"Sonya who?" cried Fearless.

"Sonya foot. I can smell it from here," bellowed Mightie McDougie.

Fearless Fiona hid her face in her hands. It was a terrible joke. The room was silent. Not a twitch. Not a smile. Not a glimpse of teeth anywhere. It was almost midnight.

There was a low rumbling sound. Mightie McDougie lurched forward with his hands clapped over his

mouth. His body was shaking like a
sack of custard.

Suddenly he threw back his head.

A tremendous hoot of laughter blew out of his mouth and turned into a deafening whistle.

Fearless Fiona stared at him. There was a huge gap between his front teeth. The whistle was what the peacocks had been waiting to hear. They ran into the room and clustered around Mightie McDougie's feet. They

sat on his shoulders.

One even perched on his head.

Fearless stared at Mightie
McDougie.

Mightie McDougie stared at
Fearless.

"It's you!" cried Fearless. "You're the
rightful Haggis!"

Mightie McDougie was
dumbfounded. A hundred years is a
long time, and things get forgotten.

Mind you, thought Fearless later, to forget something like that, you'd have to be pretty thick. Rather like the Haggis who had chucked the key in the loch in the first place. So, maybe it ran in the family . . .

On the dot of midnight, she thrust the key into Mightie McDougie's hand. And something extraordinary happened. The minute he held the key, Mightie McDougie changed

completely. He became the Earl of Haggis. He stood to his full height with his huge shoulders squared.

"Step up all those whose real name is Haggis!" bellowed the new Earl. Fearless watched in amazement as the man with the moustache, the man in the bowler hat and the woman in the leopard skin moved forward. Even

Clarence Rainbird shuffled forward. Such was the power of the rightful Haggis over the Haggis clan.

Then Mightie McDougie turned his bright blue eyes on Nigel Pug and Slimeball. The so-called Cindy Haggis was nowhere to be seen.

He raised his sword and pointed to the cellar. "Lock them up," he cried. "I shall deal with them later."

The cellar was dark and smelly. "What about our supper?" yelled Nigel Pug.

Crystal Rainbird threw a large paper bag at him.

"They doesn't deserve food!" cried the Earl of Haggis.

"They deserve this!" said Crystal Rainbird.

"*Crunchy Lunches* cookbook, page 31, Edible Dormouse patties."

"Oh, no," screamed Nigel Pug. "Not them! *Anything* but them!"

There was a strange choking and squelching as the two cheats stumbled down the steps and the cellar door was bolted shut.

Mightie McDougie, candlestick in hand, spoke in a deep voice.

"Friends and relatives," he said. "Haggis House is saved. The Tartan Traveller will continue to be a nice place for nice people to stay. But there is one thing you must all know." He turned and held the enormous candlestick high. "Without Fearless Fiona Metalpress, none of this could have happened," he said gravely. "From this day on, she is an honorary member of the Haggis clan."

There was a round of applause. Mrs

Metalpress puffed herself up like a proud mother hen and beamed around the room.

Fearless Fiona, star reporter, ran to the door. A telephone was ringing and she knew which one it was.

She grabbed the mobile phone from its clip on her

mountain bike.

"Did ya get the story?" shouted
Deadline Metalpress. Fearless could
imagine him, feet on his desk, a
notebook just like hers in his hand. She
sat down on a pile of peacock feathers
and leaned back against the Great
Stone Haggis.

"I got it," she said.

"You're the greatest," growled
Deadline Metalpress.

"You can count, on me, chief, er,
Dad," said Fearless Fiona, with a grin.

The Rolls-Royce Racket Mystery

Chapter One

"Whaddyamean your Rolls-Royce has been stolen?"

Deadline Metalpress, editor of the *Daily Screamer*, yelled to Cyril Booby the Mayor. "You don't have a Rolls-Royce!"

"I don't," wailed the Mayor. "That is to say I didn't but then I did because I borrowed it."

"Whoozwassit?" roared Deadline.

"That's the problem," whimpered the Mayor. "I borrowed it from the Queen and she wants it back tomorrow."

"WHAT?" Deadline Metalpress shot into the air. His head hit the ceiling with a bang.

His secretary opened the door. "Did you bang, sir?" she asked sweetly.

"You bet I did," roared Deadline Metalpress. "Get me Fearless Fiona. FAST!"

Fearless Fiona was Deadline's only

daughter. When other little girls played with pastry cutters and dolly tea cups, Fearless was writing the front page of the *Daily Screamer*. Deadline used to say she could dig a story up from reinforced concrete. Now she had a bike with a portable telephone. It was Deadline's idea. News travels fast, he said. You gotta move faster.

And now that phone was ringing.

Fearless Fiona looked over her shoulder to make sure she was alone. There was a fizzy feeling in her stomach. She knew something big was about to happen.

"What's up, Dad, er Chief?" she said, pulling her notebook from her back pocket.

"Someone's stolen the Mayor's Rolls-Royce,"

Deadline Metalpress yelled.

Fearless looked puzzled. "But the Mayor doesn't have a—" she began.

"He borrowed it," shouted Deadline. "The Circus is in town. He wanted to show off."

Fearless smiled to herself. Every year the Magnificent Gatuso came to town with his Circus and a brand new Rolls-Royce. Every year the Mayor sulked and personally wrote out hundreds of extra parking tickets because his official car was a rusty Morris Minor.

"Whose Rolls was it?" asked Fearless.

Deadline sucked in his breath. "The Queen's," he said. "And she wants it back, tomorrow."

Fearless felt her stomach turn over. She'd been right. It *was* something big.

She imagined the dungeons in the Tower of London. They must be damp and pretty smelly. The Mayor wouldn't like it there one little bit.

"We've got to find the Queen's Rolls-Royce, Fearless," said Deadline. "This could be our biggest story ever."

Fearless Fiona snapped her notebook shut. There was no time to lose. "You can count on me, chief," she said. Then she climbed on her bike and raced into town.

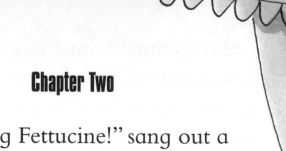

Chapter Two

"Hey! Flying Fettucine!" sang out a voice, rich and brown as chocolate sauce. "Why you not say hello to the Magnificent Gatuso?"

A huge man with a glossy black moustache stood in front of a yellow Circus tent. He was wearing a gold bath cap, red satin swimming trunks and he was washing a lime green Rolls-Royce that had orange speed stripes painted down the sides.

Fearless stopped her bike and walked over to him.

"Bellissima!" cried the Magnificent Gatuso, shaking her hand with a warm soapy grip.

Fearless laughed. She knew he was talking about his car. "It's lovely, Gatuso," she said. "I, um, love the colour."

Gatuso beamed. "I choose it especially," he said. Then he leaned forward and whispered in her ear. "It is almost the same as the Queen's."

The smile froze on Fearless's face. The Magnificent Gatuso raised the black eyebrows that hung like satin sashes over his big brown face. "Whatever is the matter, my serious spaghettini?" he cried. "Why should the Magnificent Gatuso not have the Rolls-Royce of his dreams?"

Fearless Fiona blushed and took a deep breath. "I'm sorry Gatuso," she said quickly. "It's just that, well, there are car thieves in town and . . ."

The Magnificent Gatuso threw down the sponge he was holding.

"Every town the Circus visits, these car thieves visit too," he cried. He waved his right hand in front of her. "Look at this!"

Fearless noticed a long length of chain which went round Gatuso's wrist at one end and through the steering wheel of the Rolls-Royce at the other. "I take no chances," he said, staring hard at her. "Something funny is going on."

"What do you think it is?" said Fearless.

The Magnificent Gatuso threw back his head and laughed. Rows of teeth gleamed like new bars of soap.

"I do not know, my little lasagna," he cried. "But I am thinking you will before too long."

Fearless climbed back on her bike. "I hope you're right," she said.

Her first stop was Joe's pizza parlour. She parked and walked through the glass doors up to the long chrome counter.

"Hi, Fearless," said Joe, as he spread eight different toppings on eight different pizzas. "How's things?"

Fearless pulled up a stool. "That's what I want to ask you," she said.

Joe delivered

pizzas all over town. If anything was happening, he knew about it.

Fearless bought a lemon-chocolate milkshake and slid it across the counter towards him. "Got a couple of minutes?"  Joe poured the milkshake down his throat. "Just back from the police station," he said. "Taking the usual spicy sausage and peanut butter with extra pineapple to the Inspector."

"Oh, yeah," said Fearless trying not to feel sick. "Have you heard anything about some car thieves?"

Joe leaned forward. "Sure have," he said. "They call themselves Stolen Cars for Special Occasions and there's a huge fuss because they've nicked the Mayor's Rolls."

"It's not his," said Fearless grimly. "It's the Queen's. And she wants it back tomorrow."

Joe choked. Lemon–chocolate milkshake sprayed all over the chrome counter. But Fearless wasn't listening. She was already on her way out.

Chapter Three

The Town Hall was a tall white building on the other side of the park from the Circus. The Mayor and Mayoress lived in a large flat on the ground floor.

The Mayoress was a founder member of the Dynamic Dowagers Association, which was a kind of club for Glamorous Grannies who were really bossy and not particulary pretty. In the summer she made all the clerks and typists in the Town Hall move into one office, so she could rent the rest of it for Bed & Breakfast.

Fearless walked up to the front door and banged the brass knocker. The door opened. Behind it stood a woman with long skinny legs and a face like a seagull with too much lipstick. "Oh," said the Mayoress, coldy. "I was expecting someone else."

Fearless introduced herself and smiled politely. "I wonder if I might speak to the Mayor," she asked.

The Mayoress stared at her. "I suppose so," she said. She led Fearless down a dark corridor and into a room overlooking the garden. Then she threw open the window and blew a sharp blast on a whistle hanging around her neck.

At the far end of the garden, a little man emerged from a shed and began to shuffle up the path towards the house.

"Don't be long," said the Mayoress. "Some Very Important Customers are staying." She picked up a tin of polish and began to spray the radiators.

"Dwayne and Dolores Delish. They're movie stars. I expect you've heard of them."

Fearless hadn't heard of them. She opened her notebook. "May I ask when you last saw the Queen's Rolls-Royce?" she said.

"There!" cried the Mayoress.

"Where?" said Fearless Fiona, trying not to choke on the overpowering smell of wax.

"There!" said the Mayoress, again. "Now Dwayne and Dolores will think an army of cleaners had been working for a week."

Before Fearless could reply, a woman with long hair hanging over her shoulders like strings of liquorice poured herself into the room. "It's so cute. I just love it!" she screamed.

Fearless stared as the woman spun around. She was wearing fishnet stockings and a mauve and yellow dress made out of some shiny material. Something large and gold glittered around her neck.

It was the Mayor's chain of office!

The Mayoress's beaky face went pink with pleasure. It wasn't a particularly pretty sight. "Dolores, you look sensational," she gushed. Then in a voice as sticky as melted-down sherbet, she said, "Have you spoken to your producer yet?"

Fearless watched Dolores' face go blank. "My producer?" she said.

Behind her stood a man wearing a suit that was too tight. He had a thin mouth that looked as if it had been stamped on his face. "You remember," he said, glaring at her. His eyes were hard and beady, like a crab's. "The producer who wants the Mayoress to come to Hollywood and star in his next movie."

"Why of course, I talked to him," cried Dolores a little too loudly. "And you've been so kind. Lending me this

old necklace and taking us with you to Lord and Lady Mothproof's party today."

"When do I go?" shrieked the Mayoress.

"Go?" said Dolores.

"To Hollywood!" screeched the Mayoress. Her beaky face had changed from pink to purple.

"Soon," murmured Dwayne. He took Dolores by the arm and pushed her towards the door. "We'll tell you all about it tomorrow."

As the door closed, the Mayoress began to sing in a high squeaky voice, "There's no business like show business." Then she picked up the tin of polish and began absent mindedly spraying the windows. She seemed to

have forgotten there was anyone else in the room.

"About the Mayor's Rolls-Royce," Fearless began again.

The Mayoress stopped singing and glared at her. "What about it?"

"It's disappeared, pet," whimpered the Mayor who had crept into the room. "I haven't had a moment to tell you."

"Really, Cyril," said the Mayoress sharply. "When are you going to learn

to look after your own things? I can't
go around picking up after you at
your age." She banged down the tin of
polish. "And don't call me pet in front
of strangers. You know I don't like it."

The door slammed shut.

For a moment there was silence.
Then the Mayor turned to Fearless.
"Do think it will be damp and smelly
in the Tower of London?"

Chapter Four

Half an hour later, Fearless Fiona was on her way home. All the Mayor could tell her was that he had left the keys on a hook by the back door. Anyone could have taken them. She sighed. Finding the Queen's Rolls-Royce in time was beginning to look pretty hopeless. Something had to turn up. And soon.

She turned a corner into the tree-lined street where she lived. All the houses were either made of brick with roses growing up their walls or stone, covered in ivy.

All of them that is—except for one.

Deadline Metalpress had firm ideas about the outside of his house.

It was painted in his favourite colours after one of his favourite jokes.

It was black and white and red all over. Just like a newspaper. Fearless Fiona thought it was wonderful. Just looking at it made her feel better.

Something would turn up.

She parked her bike and walked into the kitchen.

It was like walking into a vegetable catalogue.

Mrs Metalpress had firm views on decoration, too. She liked lots of it.

The wallpaper was criss-crossed with cucumbers. The curtains were covered in tomatoes. There were pumpkins on every other floor tile and the tablecloth was covered in strawberries.

"Fiona Jane!" shrieked Mrs Metalpress. She was standing at the sink carving carrots into goldfish shapes. "I've won the Hot Tips competition in my Happy Households Magazine!"

"That's terrific, Mum," said Fearless. "What was it?"

"Well," said Mrs Metalpress, taking a deep breath. "You had to send in suggestions for running a happy house and—"

"I mean, what was your tip," said Fearless, trying to look interested.

Mrs Metalpress beamed. It wasn't often her daughter wanted to know the secrets of running a happy household. "Something I learned many years ago," she said, puffing herself up just a little. "If you are expecting important visitors and want your house to smell as if an army of cleaners—"

"You spray wax on the radiators," interrupted Fearless Fiona with a grin.

Mrs Metalpress was dumbstruck.

Her eyes glazed over. She began to see her daughter in an entirely different light. Her mind filled with pictures of the two of them choosing curtains, making jam . . .

Fearless saw the danger signals immediately. Straight away she changed the subject.

"What did you win?" she said quickly.

Mrs Metalpress sighed. The visions melted away.

"That's the problem," she said. "The first prize is a helicopter ride and you know I hate heights."

There was a ring at the door. "That will be the pilot now," said Mrs Metalpress. A smile spread over her face. "You'd better go with him."

Now it was Fearless Fiona's turn to be dumbstruck. A helicopter ride! She had never been in a helicopter before! If they flew over town she might even see a clue to the missing Rolls-Royce. Maybe it was the break she had been hoping for!

Her eyes lit up. "Thanks, Mum," she said.

As she ran to the door she made a decision.

It wasn't easy.

She would let her mother teach her to knit after all.

Chapter Five

The helicopter pilot was called Fred. Fearless jumped into his car and they drove to the airfield.

The helicopter blades were already whirling round when they arrived. Fred fiddled with dials and pulled knobs. "Where do you want to go?" he asked.

Everything she knew about the missing Rolls-Royce went through Fearless's mind. Suddenly her bloodhound's nose for a story began to twitch. She said, "Do you know where Lord and Lady Mothproof live?"

Fred nodded.

A minute later they were flying over Mothproof Hall. Fearless pulled out her binoculars. The first thing she saw were two girls in white sacks sitting in the stone birdbaths on either side of the front door. Her heart sank. She didn't have to look at their faces. She knew who they were.

Crinoline and Lacy were the daughters of Lord and Lady Mothproof. The were also the wettest weeds in the world. Only last week Fearless had been forced to go to tea with them. She shuddered at the memory.

Fred looked down. "What on earth are they doing?" he asked.

Fearless was almost too embarrassed to tell him.

It was so unbelievably soppy and it was one of their favourite games. "They're pretending to be soft-boiled eggs," she muttered.

Fred grunted but said nothing.

There was nothing to say.

They flew around the back of the house where there was a huge courtyard. There were lots of cars parked outside.

"There must be a party going on," said Fred.

Then Fearless remembered Dolores Delish in her mauve and yellow dress wearing the Mayor's chain of office. "Let's have a closer look," she said.

They circled low over the courtyard. In one corner underneath a roof of vines sat Lord Mothproof's huge purple Rolls-Royce. It was exactly the same colour as the grapes which hung in bunches all around it. Fearless peered carefully through the binoculars. There was no sign of any car thieves. Nothing she could see looked even slightly suspicious.

She felt confused. She had followed her nose and and she had been wrong. It had never happened before.

"How about flying over the Circus?" said Fred.

"Okay," said Fearless glumly.

She stared down at the park. A moment later the Circus tent appeared. Around it she could see the circus people's caravans and all the animal pens.

Then one caravan caught her eye. It was painted gold and looked much flashier than any of the others and was surrounded on all sides by a high fence. A T-shirt flapped on a clothes line outside it.

"Stop!" cried Fearless Fiona.

"Don't be silly," said Fred.

Fearless blushed. "Sorry," she said. "Could you fly a bit lower over that gold caravan?"

Fred dropped down. This time the writing on the T-shirt was completely clear. In large blue letters, it said

Fearless Fiona's heart went bang in her chest!

She pulled out her binoculars. Written along the side of the caravan in glittering rhinestones were the letters LL.

"Where now?" asked Fred.

"Home," said Fearless Fiona. "As fast as possible."

Suddenly there was everything to go for!

Chapter Six

By the time Fearless collected her bicycle and pedalled back to the Circus, it was beginning to get dark.

The Magnificent Gatuso was still outside. Except now he was rubbing handfuls of wax onto his already gleaming Rolls-Royce.

"Aha!" he cried when he saw Fearless running across the grass towards him. "It is my restless ravioli! Always in a hurry! Always asking questions!" He put down his polish. "I, the Magnificent Gatuso, have a question to ask you."

"What is it, Gatuso?" said Fearless, looking startled.

The Magnificent Gatuso wiped his

hands on his red satin shorts.

He paused. "What do you think of my car?" he asked and he laughed until tears ran down his face.

Fearless laughed too. Then in a serious voice, she said. "Gatuso, I need to know who lives in the gold caravan."

"Ah," said the Magnificent Gatuso, flicking a large polishing cloth out of his back pocket. "That would be Len and Lucy, the elephant keepers."

Fearless Fiona's eyes narrowed. "Have they been with the circus for long?" she asked.

"So many questions, my searching semolina!" cried the Magnficent Gatuso. "No, they are not with the Circus very long I think."

"Would you mind if I look around?" said Fearless.

The Magnificent Gatuso shrugged. "Of course not," he said. "Right now, Len and Lucy rehearse in the big tent."

Fearless lifted the heavy flap and peered inside. The tent was lit up with strings of tiny white lights hanging in loops from the ceiling. Brass band music was playing and in the middle of the tent six elephants bumped around a ring holding on to each others' tails.

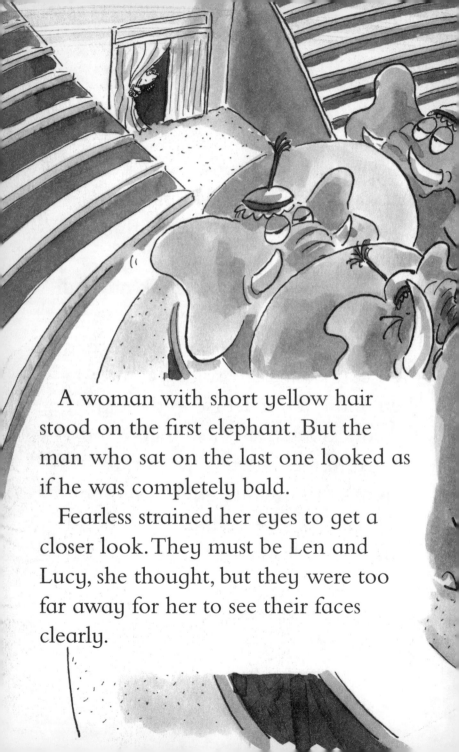

A woman with short yellow hair stood on the first elephant. But the man who sat on the last one looked as if he was completely bald.

Fearless strained her eyes to get a closer look. They must be Len and Lucy, she thought, but they were too far away for her to see their faces clearly.

Fearless walked behind the tent into the cluster of animal pens and caravans. It was almost dark now. All around her were strange grunts and snuffles from animals she couldn't see. Suddenly the music in the tent stopped. The rehearsal was over.

Fearless knew she had to investigate the gold caravan before Len and Lucy saw her.

The ground shuddered under her feet as the elephants were led out of the tent. In front of her was a narrow alley between two snorting pens. She took a deep breath and ran down it.

At that moment, the moon came out. At the end of the alley was a glint of something bright between the slats of a high fence.

It was the gold caravan!

She ran towards it and quickly climbed the fence. The clothes line was still there but the T-shirt had gone. Fearless tried the door. It was locked. Curtains were drawn across the windows.

On the other side of the fence, came the sound of voices. There was no time to lose. She climbed out and stood facing a huge pile of straw. Beside it was the outline of a tall pen which Fearless guessed must be for the elephants.

She pulled out her pencil torch and flicked it quickly over the grass. Nothing. She was just about to put it back when something square and shiny by the straw caught her eye. She flashed the torch on it. It was a silver card. It said:

Treat Yourself to B&B at the
Town Hall
"We're the Best - Stuff the Rest"
Geranium Booby,
(Mayoress)

The voices grew nearer. Fearless put the card in her pocket, ran back to her bicycle and pedalled into town.

There was someone she had to see immediately.

Fearless hadn't planned to stop at the pizza parlour. But she saw Joe through the window wildly waving his arms at her.

"Fearless!" he cried. "Thank goodness, I saw you! Lord Mothproof's Rolls has been stolen!"

"When?" said Fearless.

"This afternoon," said Joe, sliding a pizza into a large flat box. "The Mayor's just telephoned. He was going to give it to the Queen in place of her Rolls-Royce. And now they've both been nicked."

Fearless Fiona looked at the box. "Is that for the Town Hall?" she said quickly.

Joe nodded. "The Mayoress's usual," he said. "Salty cod lumps with sour pickles."

Fearless grabbed the box. "I'll deliver it," she said. And she raced out the door.

Five minutes later she was in the Town Hall walking into the room overlooking the garden. She put the pizza down on the table.

"Can't you see I'm too upset to eat?" said a sulky voice. It was the Mayoress.

She was sitting on the sofa, pushing chocolates into her beaky face.

The Mayor was staring out of the window absent-mindedly pulling on a strand of wool attached to his jersey. His jersey was slowly disappearing. He turned to the Mayoress. "Worst of all worlds," he whispered. "I didn't think you cared."

The Mayoress sat up with a jerk.

"I wasn't talking about you, Cyril," she snapped. "I was talking about Dwayne and Dolores." She fell back on the sofa with a sob. "They're leaving tomorrow morning."

"What about me?" wailed the Mayor. "Now Lord Mothproof's Rolls-Royce has been stolen, too. I've got nothing to give the Queen." He gulped and held up a ragged arm to his forehead. "I'll be dragged in chains to a damp smelly dungeon."

Suddenly the Mayoress sat up. "What do you want?" she snapped at Fearless.

Fearless took a deep breath. It was now or never.

"Have you been to the circus recently?" she asked.

"What a ridiculous question,"

snapped the Mayoress. "Absolutely not."

"Thank you," said Fearless. "That's all I wanted to know."

The Mayoress shrugged and stuffed another chocolate in her mouth.

The Mayor shuffled across the floor towards Fearless. All that was left of his jersey were the cuffs. He put out his hand. "I want to thank you for trying to help," he said.

"Don't thank me yet," said Fearless Fiona with a determined smile on her face. "Meet me outside the Circus with Lord Mothproof first thing tomorrow morning."

On her way home, Fearless stopped and steered her bike behind a hedge. She looked over both shoulders to make sure no one was watching her. Then she picked up her portable telephone.

"Whaddyawant?" yelled Deadline Metalpress, editor of the *Daily Screamer*.

When Fearless told him, his eyes almost popped out of his head. "When for?" he bawled.

"First thing tomorrow morning," said Fearless Fiona.

Chapter Seven

It was early in the morning. The Magnificent Gatuso was standing in his grey silk pyjamas and staring at the huge crowd of people gathering in the park.

"Hey Gatuso!" yelled Joe. He was weaving in and out of the crowd on his bicycle, balancing boxes and boxes of pizzas. "The Queen's coming! Want a Royal Relish Breakfast Special?"

"The Queen is coming?" cried the Magnificent Gatuso in total amazement. "The

Queen is coming to my Circus? Mama
Mia! Whoopsie Daisy!"

There was a dull thud and a flutter
of grey silk. The Magnificent Gatuso
had fainted.

"I say, look at that," creaked a voice
like a rusty hinge. Lord Mothproof was
standing in an old raincoat that came
down to his ankles. He prodded the
Mayor with his umbrella. "One of the
baby elephants has fallen over."

Beside him, the Mayor was shaking
like a leaf, hoping against hope that
the Queen might have got her dates
mixed up. "Help me, Lord Mothproof,"
he gibbered. "What am I going to
say?"

Lord Mothproof looked puzzled for a
minute. "How about, there, there, baby
elephant," he suggested.

The Mayor opened his mouth to reply but only a strange gargling noise came out.

Lord Mothproof watched him out of the corner of his eye. Silly little man, he thought. Can't look after the Queen's Rolls-Royce. Doesn't know what to say to elephants. He prodded him again with his umbrella. "Look here," he said. "Where's Fearless Fiona? She's the one you need."

"She's on her way," muttered the Mayor. Which wasn't true because he had been looking for Fearless all morning. She seemed to have completely disappeared.

"Excuse me, sir," said a voice underneath a blue helmet. "Message from the Inspector. Her Majesty will be here in five minutes."

The Mayor's face went white. "Have you found Fearless Fiona yet?" he croaked.

The policeman shook his head.

"We'll keep looking," he said. The Mayor stared hopelessly in front of him. Thoughts of damp, smelly dungeons filled his head.

WHERE WAS FEARLESS FIONA?

"CYRIL!" shrieked a voice like a thousand lightbulbs shattering.

"I've been cheated!" The Mayoress barrelled through the crowd. Her beaky face was black with rage. "Those so-called movie-stars," she screeched.

"They never left a phone number. They didn't even pay their bill. If I ever get my hands on them!"

An enormous sigh rippled through the crowd as a scarlet and gold coach pulled by four white horses rolled slowly down the street and stopped.

The Mayor stood frozen to the spot. A truly terrible thought had occurred to him. It was bad enough to lose the Queen's Rolls-Royce but in his worst dreams it had never occurred to him that it might be the only one she had.

He watched horrified as a long red carpet unrolled across the grass towards him. The coach door opened.

WHERE WAS FEARLESS FIONA?

Whocka-whocka-whocka!

Out of nowhere a helicopter swooped over the circus!

The Mayor looked up. So did Lord Mothproof. So did the Magnificent Gatuso who was now fully recovered and dressed in a flowing black cape.

Beside the pilot, dressed in her white leather catsuit, was Fearless Fiona!

grapes. The other was a rich glossy silver with three gold letters on the numberplate – HRH.

It was the Queen's Rolls-Royce!

Fearless jumped down from the helicopter and ran across the flattened grass.

Behind the wheel of the silver car was a man with a thin smile and a bald head. It was Dwayne Delish – alias Len the elephant keeper!

Behind the wheel of the other was Dolores Delish. Fearless watched as she snatched a black wig from her head – Dolores Delish disappeared.

Lucy sat at the wheel! She was

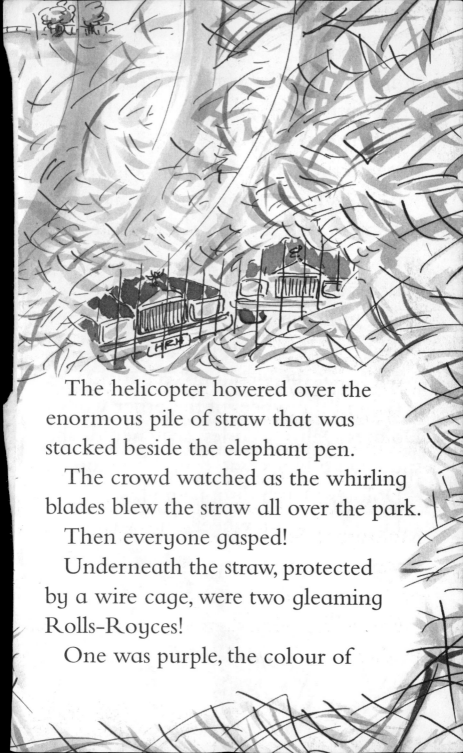

The helicopter hovered over the
enormous pile of straw that was
stacked beside the elephant pen.

The crowd watched as the whirling
blades blew the straw all over the park.

Then everyone gasped!

Underneath the straw, protected
by a wire cage, were two gleaming
Rolls-Royces!

One was purple, the colour of

wearing a T-shirt which said STOLEN
CARS FOR SPECIAL OCCASIONS
in large blue letters.

Fearless raced towards the cage.

A short tunnel of wire led onto
the road. She could hear the throaty
roar as the two Rolls-Royces moved
forward.

A low snarl came from the crowd.

There was a flash of a long black
cape.

Fearless watched in amazement as
the Mayoress and the Magnificent
Gatuso shot down the tunnel. The
Rolls-Royces were roaring towards
them. For one terrible moment it
looked as if the thieves were going to
escape!

Suddenly the Magnificent Gatuso

threw his huge black cape over
the windscreen of the Queen's
Rolls-Royce.

At the same moment the Mayoress
whipped out her tin of polish and
sprayed wax all over the windscreen of
Lord Mothproof's Rolls Royce.

Both cars screeched to a halt.

The huge crowd clapped and
cheered.

There was no need to call the police.

By the time the Mayoress had finished
with Dwayne and Dolores Delish
– alias Len and Lucy – they were
more than happy to go to jail.

As Fearless wandered across the grass
to buy herself a candyfloss, a phone
began to ring. She ran to where her
bike was strapped to the side of the
helicopter.

"Mayor's just telephoned," yelled

Deadline Metalpress. "Queen knows everything!"

"What's up?" said Fearless a little nervously.

"*Daily Screamer* **by Royal Appointment,**" bellowed Deadline Metalpress in a voice so loud, that Fearless nearly dropped the phone. "Fearless, you're the greatest!"

Fearless felt hot and flushed, she was so proud. "You can count on me, Chief, er Dad," she said with a huge smile on her face.